JEANNE-MARIE
AT THE FAIR

by

Françoise

Charles Scribner's Sons   New York

"Good morning flowers!
Good morning birds!"
Jeanne-Marie opens her window very early.
Is it a fine day?
Yes! The sky is all pink.

Today Jeanne-Marie is going
to the village fair.
How excited she is!

Jeanne-Marie dresses herself.
Then she goes downstairs
and has her breakfast.
She has bread and butter
and milk with a little coffee in it.
Before she leaves the house
she makes her bed, carefully.

Patapon, her pet sheep, watches her.
Everywhere that Jeanne-Marie goes
Patapon must go too.

And off to the fair Jeanne-Marie goes
with her father on the scooter.
"Have lots of fun"
Mother calls from the window.
It's a beautiful day,
the sun is shining.
The birds are singing
"Cui-cui-cui!"

But Patapon does not go!
Before she left,
Jeanne-Marie tied her to a tree,
in the field where the daisies are white
and the sun shines all day long.
"Stay there, Patapon,"
said Jeanne-Marie.
"Sheep do not go to the fair,
except to be sold.
And I do not want you to be sold.
Wait for me, Patapon."

At the fair
it's so gay!
Music here—music there,
music everywhere.
Jeanne-Marie goes on all
the merry-go-rounds—
On a pink pig
On a huge yellow lion
Then—in an airplane.

Up in the air
Up in the air
Jeanne-Marie flies.

After a time
Jeanne-Marie is a little dizzy.
So she leaves the merry-go-round,
and walks on.

The man at the gingerbread stall calls:
"Come buy your gingerbread pig!
I'll christen it for you in a minute.
Come buy your gingerbread pig!"

So Jeanne-Marie buys a gingerbread pig.
The man writes on it in pink sugar

Jeanne-Marie walks on,
all through the fair.
And all of a sudden
she meets—her great friend Jean Pierre.
Jean Pierre buys her a big red balloon.
Then he takes her to the café.
"Will you have some orangeade
Jeanne-Marie"?

Hum-m-m! How good it is!

Now she has had her orangeade,
and eaten her gingerbread pig.
Jeanne-Marie tries her luck
at the wheel that turns.
Round and round goes the wheel.

The lucky number will win a prize.

Jeanne-Marie has won!
Her prize is a great big
DOLL!
A baby doll dressed all in pink.

Jeanne-Marie hugs her,
and the doll says,
in such a funny little voice:
"Pa-pa!"
"Mam-a!"

Meanwhile Patapon is tired of being alone
in the green field.
She too, would like to go to the fair.
And why not?
She pulls and pulls on her rope.
The rope breaks.
She is free!
So she finds the road to the village
and she runs—and runs...
When she sees houses she runs faster.
She does not want anyone to send her
back to the farm.

And at last—she is at the fair!

Where is Jeanne-Marie?
Patapon looks everywhere.
She looks, and looks.
Then Madame Fatima, who tells fortunes,
calls her.
"Little sheep," she says,
"I see in my cards that you are looking
for your little mistress, Jeanne-Marie.
Go to the circus—quickly—
I know that she is there."

"Beh-beh-beh"
"Thank you, Madame,"
says Patapon most politely.

Patapon goes on looking.
She goes to all the merry-go-rounds,
and all the little shops
that sell toys and cakes.
She bleats loudly. "Be-e-e-e-ee-ee!"
"Jeanne-Marie, where are you?
Jeanne-Marie-ee-ee!"

Then all tired out with crying,
Patapon goes to the big circus.
As she gets nearer she hears fine music,
Boum-Boum-Boum,
Tra-la-la-la-la!

And there in the very middle of the circus,
Patapon sees an enormous animal.
It is gray and wrinkled, with big ears.
In place of a nose it has a long trunk,
swinging from side to side.
Patapon is so scared!
She bleats—
and bleats and bleats—desperately.
"Be-e-e-e-ee-ee!"
"Jeanne-Marie-Marie-ee-ee!"

Jeanne-Marie
hearing the beloved little voice
rushes to help.
Then the elephant gives the little sheep
a friendly pat on the head—with his trunk.

But Patapon is still scared
and wants to go home.
It is late, and everyone is leaving the fair.
Patapon rides in the new trailer.
Scooters are a little dangerous for dolls,
and so Jean Pierre's father
takes the baby doll in his car.

Next day Jeanne-Marie will have the doll,
safe and fresh and rosy.

Now they are asleep.
Jeanne-Marie dreams
of her doll.
And Patapon dreams
of that big gray animal.
In her dreams she is brave...
But never will she forget
that elephant.
Never!